# THE MYSTERY

## OF THE SEVEN STANES

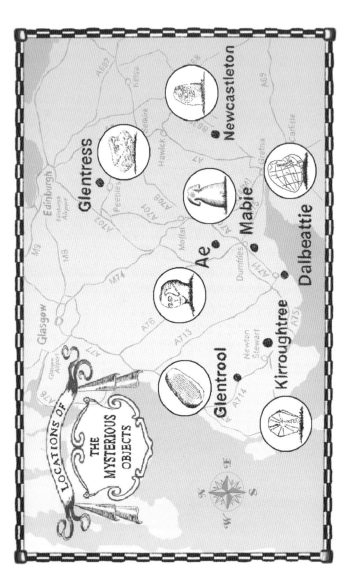

A tree is beautiful, but what's more, it has a right to life; like water, the sun and the stars, it is essential. Life on earth is inconceivable without trees. Forests create climate, climate influences peoples' character, and so on and so forth. There can be neither civilization nor happiness if forests crash down under the axe, if the climate is harsh and severe, people are also harsh and severe....
What a terrible future!

*Anton Pavlovich Chekhov (1860-1904)*

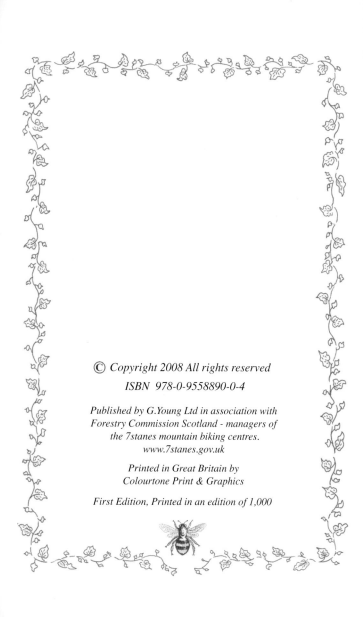

ISBN 978-0-9558890-0-4

Published by G.Young Ltd in association with
Forestry Commission Scotland - managers of
the 7stanes mountain biking centres.
www.7stanes.gov.uk

Printed in Great Britain by
Colourtone Print & Graphics

First Edition, Printed in an edition of 1,000

# Contents

# Introduction

Professor Ralph Deeson WMD. KLM.

When those fine chaps at The Forestry Commission asked me if I would be interested in investigating seven boulders, uncovered whilst building their mountain bike trails, I wondered if they had contacted the right person. My own particular specialty is pre-bronze age archaeology and as the seven unidentified objects all had some form of inscription on them, I assumed they were from a later period. Therefore I was unsure if my field of endeavour was applicable to the task at hand. I was considering whether or not to take on the assignment when some photographs of the artefacts fell through my letterbox. They appeared to be rather diverse in nature and I wondered why The Forestry Commission considered them to be connected as a group. It was only when I saw the detailed inscriptions on each object that I could see they were indeed connected. All the objects were in remarkably good condition considering they had been buried for so long. As I was extremely curious to discover what they were and who on

Earth could have put them there, I decided to accept the challenge. I resolved to grasp the thistle by the horns, as it were, and throwing the proverbial caution to the wind, take up the glorious quest of solving the 'Mystery of the Seven Stanes'.

The mesmerising science of Archaeology has been my passion since I was a young boy. I seem to have inherited this passion from my Father, the late Humphrey D. Deeson, who was a keen amateur archaeologist. I fondly remember, at the tender age of seven, being transfixed when he showed me a photograph of the magnificent bust of Nefertiti. The literal translation of her name is "The beautiful woman has come". I was enchanted by the artistry of her effigy and enthralled that such a beautiful ancient object could have been dug out of the earth in such pristine condition. Her one remaining glass eye cast a magical spell on my young mind, which remains with me to this day. When Father showed me that picture, I had a eureka moment. Like Archimedes I had discovered something extraordinary. I had discovered my vocation.

Archaeology, from the Greek: archaios, meaning 'ancient' and logos, meaning 'knowledge', is the study of human cultures through the recovery of their remains. Its goals are to document and explain the origins and development of human culture. The methodology employed is to retrieve, analyse then document the artefacts produced by past civilizations. It is a science of deduction, a science of puzzle solving. You are given a number of clues, usually in the form of objects or artefacts, and from them you have to deduce what they were used for and what kind of society produced them. It is often asked why archaeologists are obsessed with the past; why they rummage around in the dirt, with their little trowels, looking at scraps of pottery. A cynic would ask why not forget about the past and concentrate on the future? I would stem that cynical outburst by pointing out that if humanity has an understanding of its past, then it is less likely to repeat the failures of that past. In essence the purpose behind the glorious endeavour of archaeology is to increase humanity's sum knowledge of itself. A wonderful endeavour for any high-spirited lad or lassie to pursue.

At a more mundane level archaeology fulfils a basic human instinct, the instinct to be curious. Mankind or womankind, for there is no gender bias in this trait, is essentially a curious animal. That curiosity has been instrumental in bringing our species from the treetops to the technologically driven societies of our wonderfully modern world. To put it simply, human beings are curious about being human beings. If by studying past cultures we can find out a little more about ourselves then it is indeed an extremely worthwhile endeavour. Undoubtedly it can be seen as a glorious quest.

To broaden the investigation of the Mystery of the Seven Stanes I took the liberty of asking Professor G.R. Plumpton to join me on this intriguing quest. He is an eminent professor of anthropology, well respected in his field, and I thought his expertise would be invaluable to the project. We spent a period of just over three months investigating these seven unidentified large objects and here, set before you, are the results.

Professor Plumpton suggested that, for the sake of an accurate representation, we should abbreviate the seven large unidentified objects to. S.L.U.O. As I hate the modern habit of using acronyms for almost everything U.T.S. (Under The Sun) I shall refrain from implementing his suggestion. From here on, I will simply refer to the seven unidentified objects as 'The Objects'.

The document in your hand is compiled from my field notes, which I have summarised into a series of chapters, each one dealing with an individual object. I have presented it in this form to allow you, dear reader, to follow our progress as we unravel the Mystery of the Seven Stanes. Even though there are some aspects of the mystery still to be resolved, I believe there is enough information presented here to give the general reader an impression of the sheer joy we experienced when discovering the seven hidden treasures. It is my sincere hope that this humble document will give you an insight into our methodology and thus open up a window that will allow you to enter the wonderful world of archaeology.

*For the benefit of the non-Scottish readers 'Stanes' is the Scottish word for stones.*

## Chapter One

## Glentress Forest

# The Meteorite

*Where Professor Deeson partakes in a generously proportioned homemade cake, discovers a gobbledygook-ridden viral object and eats too many oysters.*

When making arrangements with Professor Plumpton to visit the Seven Stanes sites, he very kindly suggested that we make use of his car. On the first morning of our expedition I was standing outside my Edinburgh residence when a magnificent chauffeur driven automobile approached. This outstanding feat of automotive engineering seemed to glide along the road before stopping in front of me, two inches from the kerb. From the back seat Professor Plumpton enthusiastically waved at me. The car was a 1959 Bentley S2 continental, a true classic. Up close its sleek well proportioned lines were a delight to behold. It had that quintessential grace present only in the best designs, like the majestic lines of a greyhound or the exquisite grace of a beautiful woman's leg. There was an

illusive element buried deep within this car's design that spoke to me of the divine being. The car's chrome was burnished to a mirror-like gleam and its paintwork was a resplendent midnight blue. Hargreaves, Professor Plumpton's chauffeur, came out and opened the passenger door for me. He was dressed in an elegant but businesslike grey suit with the traditional peaked cap and leather driving gloves of his trade. He greeted me with a clipped,

"Good morning Sir."

As I entered the car, its exuberant interior engulfed my senses. It was a symphony in red hide upholstery, luxurious deep-pile carpet and polished walnut veneer. Hargreaves assumed his driving position and then asked Professor Plumpton,

"Shall we go Sir?"

When the Professor replied in the affirmative Hargreaves switched on the 6230 cc aluminium V8 engine and it quietly purred into life. In a moment we were gliding through the beautifully proportioned streets of Scotland's capital, which seemed to have been designed for just such a car as Plumpton's Bentley. It was a perfect start to our great adventure.

As we wafted down the A70l and then on to the A703 heading south towards Peebles I asked Plumpton how he came to be in possession of such a magnificent vehicle. He told me he had inherited it from his father along with the services of Hargreaves. He then further informed me that in all the time he owned the car it had never once broken down. He attributed this remarkable reliability to the fact that Hargreaves, as well as being his chauffeur, was also an excellent car mechanic and carried out all the maintenance himself.

We drove through Peebles, which nestles snugly within an area of outstanding beauty and has been a royal burgh since 1152. It is a pretty little town cherished by locals and visitors alike for its unspoilt picturesque character. The town lies at the confluence of the River Tweed, and the Eddleston Water, locally called The Cuddy. The town's motto is "Against the Stream they Multiply" which refers to the outstanding, world renowned, salmon fishing provided by the river Tweed. Today its most striking building is the Old Parish Church that was built between 1885 and 1887 at a cost of £9,500, a tidy sum in those days. Today's Peebles

is an attractive, bustling town whose heart lies in its main shopping street, formed by High Street and Eastgate. Close by on the south side of High Street is the lovely courtyard setting of the Tweeddale Museum and Gallery, which I am assured, is well worth a visit. Initially Peebles was a market town and played a large role in the Scottish wool industry, but it has changed somewhat and is now home to a lot of people who, for some reason, commute to Edinburgh.

We left Peebles on the A72 and drove for a mile and a half towards Innerleithen where we reached the entrance to Glentress Forest. The entrance is on the left and is well sign posted. The trailhead, as the starting point for all the mountain bike trails are quaintly called, is at the lower car park, which is also known as the Osprey car park. Here we found a café and after making ourselves, comfortable I partook in a generously proportioned homemade cake and coffee, which was very reasonably priced.

Glentress lies deep in the heart of the picturesque Tweed Valley Forest Park and is one of the most diverse forests in the south of Scotland. The majestic

river Tweed can be found near its southern border. I have spent many a delightful gastronomic evening in a certain Edinburgh restaurant, which, for the benefit of its management will remain nameless, eating salmon procured from the river Tweed.

Glentress has some interesting features for the budding archaeologist, beyond the task at hand of solving the Mystery of the Seven Stanes. There is Shieldgreen Tower and the ramparts of an Iron Age hill fort on Janet's Brac from which you can view a spectacular vista of Peebles and Tweeddale. From there a short walk leads to a reconstruction of a timber round house of the Iron Age period, which. If Professor Plumpton and I were not ensconced with our glorious task; we would certainly have visited it. Glentress forest claims to have some of the largest mature Douglas Fir trees in Scotland. Some of these trees were planted in the 1920s when the forest was created to fulfil the national need for timber after the ravages of the First World War. It occurred to me when looking at one of these extraordinary specimens that there aren't many things in this God-almighty world that are more beautiful than a tree.

There's nothing like a delightful walk in the woods to experience a healthy dose of country sights, sounds and smells. Scotland now has some of the most progressive access legislation in Europe thanks to the Land Reform (Scotland) Act, which came into force in February 2005. This Act gives everyone a statutory right of responsible access to most land. Of course you can't walk through a chap's private garden or march through a farmer's crop. Nevertheless, generally speaking, you can go anywhere you please as long as you are a responsible citizen and respect the land and its owners.

After walking for two miles, we came to a vast gorge in the woods and just beyond it; we entered a secluded glade filed with Larch trees Douglas Firs and Sitka Spruce. Professor Plumpton informed me that this particular part of the forest is called the Spooky Wood. Lying above our heads, perched on a massive pile of soil lay our quarry. The first of the seven objects under our investigation, the first part of the puzzle that makes up the Seven Stanes Mystery.

At first sight the object seems to resemble a meteorite, a meteorite that has crashed into the forest

at great speed leaving behind a large track of fallen trees. It is very large and has an irregular shaped surface comprising of complex curved bumps and hollows. The object is approximately 10ft tall by 5ft 4-inches wide by 5ft thick and I would estimate it to weigh something in the region of six to seven tons. Like most of the objects we encounter along the way it has two distinct inscriptions carved into it. The first inscription is located about knee high on one side of the object and is in the form of a clue. It is important to note that this clue is one of the keys to solving the mystery, because it is similar to the clues found on the other six objects. If you want to solve the puzzle and be rewarded by having a tree planted in your name, I would suggest that you note down this inscription in the space provided at the back of this book. When you have collected all seven inscriptions you can then complete the puzzle and send it into those fine chaps at The Forestry Commission. The first clue looks like this.

The dashes represent letters that I have deliberately omitted from this publication. The reasoning behind this omission is to allow you, dear reader to find

out for yourself the joy and pleasure of solving the Mystery of the Seven Stanes.

The second inscription is in the form of a strange text which raps all around the rock like a ribbon. This is what it says.

vu'Ha'mo' nganpu',
'u''a'vaD yuQvam DoQ tlhIngan wo'.
mab mub 'oH naghvam'e'.
tugh mapaw, Sanna'lIj wIwuqta'.

As Professor Plumpton is well versed in linguistics and has been instrumental in deciphering a number of ancient texts, I asked him if he could translate it for me. After a moments hesitation he replied in a rather frustrated tone.

"Well unfortunately, I'm at a bit of a loss here. I have never come across this kind of text before." He paused to remove his hat then continued.

"As you know an alphabet is a standardized set of letters, each of which represents a phoneme of a spoken language, a phoneme being a representation of a sound within a language. This text seems to be written using the English alphabet, which I am sure you know, is derived from the twenty-six letters of

the Latin alphabet. Unfortunately the words here don't make any sense to me. The problem is that it appears, on the surface, to be an alphabetical form of linguistic gobbledygook. Having said that the Egyptian hieroglyphs were also a form of linguistic gobbledygook, until the French scholar Jean-Francois Champollion deciphered the Rosetta Stone thus unlocking their secrets in 1822. Unfortunately in this case we don't have an equivalent Rosetta Stone for this text."

He paused then proceeded to pace around the object a couple of times with the determination of a hound-dog looking for a particularly juicy bone, then continued.

"Of course language is an ever-changing amorphous beast. The American writer William Burroughs had an interesting theory about it, where he compared the behaviour of language to the behaviour of a virus. A virus that is in a constant state of mutation as it passes from person to person. There is some validity in this rather whacky theory when you consider that there are in fact thousands of varieties of English spoken in the world today. They are known to linguistics as pigeon English. With the development of worldwide communication networks

you might expect these varieties of English to be in decline, but on the contrary they are in fact increasing. It is rather amusing when you consider that globalisation is supposedly making the world a smaller place and yet language is proliferating into all sorts of weird and wonderful forms. I suppose God's wrath, when he cursed the people of Babel to speak in many tongues still plagues the world today." The esteemed Professor then paused, and after scratching his head continued.

"Anyway, if the text is a representation of some foreign language, then it is one that I have never came across. I would be extremely surprised if it is a language spoken on this Earth today. To sum up, I am afraid this text is completely alien to me and, in all honesty, I could not even hazard a guess as to what it is trying to tell us."

I was rather disappointed by the esteemed professor's negative tone but for the sake of the glorious quest I tried to retrieve the situation by saying.

"Ok, what we have before us is a large rock, which resembles a meteorite and is covered in alien writing that may be some form of virus."

"Well not exactly." The bold Professor Plumpton corrected.

"I'm not saying it's alien, I'm saying it's alien to me. Also I'm not saying it is a virus. I am suggesting that languages, all forms of languages, could be construed as being viral in nature."

Professor Plumpton then continued his hunt for the juicy bone by once again walking around the object, then asked

"Do you really think it could be a meteorite?"

"No, somehow I doubt it." I replied.

"A meteorite starts off as a meteoroid which is a heavenly body travelling through the solar system. If by some trick of fate, it enters the Earth's atmosphere the heat energy created by friction will make it glow and it is then called a meteor, or a shooting star. If it passes through the Earth's atmosphere and lands on the surface it is then called a meteorite. Meteorites are named after the place they are found, therefore if this was proven to be one it would be called The Glentress Meteorite.

The reason I doubt it to be a meteorite is that there are three different classifications of meteorites, Stony, Stony-Irons and Irons, Unfortunately the object before us does not seem to fit into any of these classifications.

If it is a meteorite then it is one which is new to science, which in itself is not such a strange idea. After all, when you consider it is a relatively new situation where humans are sending objects into space and occasionally they do come back down. Technically speaking if a piece of falling space junk reaches the Earth's surface it should be defined as a meteorite. Also there is in fact a precedent for the meteorite theory. According to the Galloway Gazette, a two-foot long meteorite landed in a Stranraer garden owned by a Mrs Agnes Lermount.

Even though my first instinct would be to rule out the possibility of this object being a large meteorite I would not dismiss the idea completely. It is important at this stage in our enquiry to keep an open mind. As my old tutor Professor D. D Pendington would say, 'An open mind is the best tool in the arsenal of any self-respecting archaeologist.'

After Professor Plumpton measured the object and took a sample for further analysis we trekked out of the forest back to the awaiting Hargreaves. Donning his obligatory driving gloves he drove us back to Auld Reekie in the flick of a lamb's tail.

That night after a late supper of oysters washed down with a rather delicate Sauvignon Blanc I was rudely woken by a strange and somewhat disconcerting dream. In it I found myself at the epicentre of a dark, brooding, forest wearing nothing but my nightshirt. It was dead of night, but the cool-blue light of a full moon eerily illuminated the trees surrounding me. As I looked up to the star encrusted jet-black sky a shooting star appeared and transfixed me like a rabbit caught in a car's headlights. This heavenly object came hurtling towards me and before I could make my escape it crashed, with an almighty thud, about two feet from my bare feet. An unearthly foreboding silence then engulfed the forest. A moment later this shocking absence of sound was filled by a hissing of steam that emanated from the object. It then started to rumble and vibrate and proceeded to break in half. Curled up inside was a fearsome man-like creature who uncoiled himself and stood before me. He must have been at least seven feet tall, had a mass of long black hair, a full beard and complementary bushy eyebrows. Set above his piercing black eyes he had a strangely furrowed forehead. He was dressed in what appeared to be some kind of uniform made from tooled leather and weapon-like instruments were

hanging from his belt. Looking me square in the eye he shouted some gobbledygook then started to laugh. When his amusement had abated he preceded to hand me a spherical glass vessel, which had the letter V engraved on its surface. I reluctantly accepted the gift but finding it too hot to handle let it drop to the forest floor. It cracked open with an acrid pop and an all-encompassing purple vapour proceeded to engulf me. Thankfully at that point I woke up in a cold sweat. When I went into the kitchen to get a glass of water to calm my nerves, I wondered if old Professor Pendington's open-minded approach to the Mystery of the Seven Stanes was such a good idea after all.

Hargreaves and the Bentley S2 Continental.

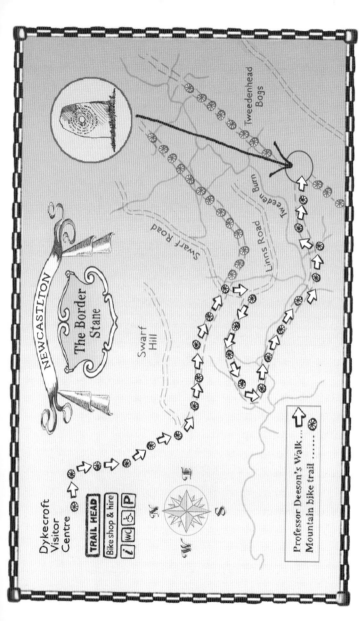

Dykecroft
Visitor
Centre

**TRAIL HEAD**
Bike shop & hire

*i* WC ♿ P

NEWCASTLTON

The Border Stane

Swarf Hill

Swarf Road

Tweeden Burn

Linns Road

Tweedenhead Bogs

N
E
S
W

Professor Deeson's Walk.... ⇧
Mountain bike trail ...... ❀

## Chapter Two

# Newcastleton Forest

# The Border Stane

*Where Professor Deeson remembers his Boy Scout training, forgetful Professor Plumpton takes a shower and they both almost sing a Scottish classic.*

On the second day of our glorious quest, I was leaving my Edinburgh residency when Mrs Postlethwaite, my housekeeper, suggested that I take my umbrella. She explained to me that even though the morning was bright with a moderate easterly breeze, the forecast stated that temperatures could reach thirteen degrees centigrade in the afternoon, but there was also a probability of light showers. This ability of Mrs. Postlethwaite's to predict the weather with such accuracy has never ceased to amaze me. As I have never known her to be wrong, I took my trusty umbrella and as I joined Professor Plumpton in the back seat of his Bentley he remarked

"I don't think you will need your brolly old chap,

it's going to be a glorious day."
I simply smiled, then reverting to
my boy scout training, said.
"Always be prepared old boy,
always be prepared."

He shook his head and we set off, heading south
toward our rendezvous with the second object in
our glorious quest.

We drove down the A7 to Hawick then took the
A6088 before turning off onto the B6357 towards
Newcastleton" In times gone by this border country
was known as "The Debatable Land", home of the
Armstrongs and the Elliots. Even the Union of the
crowns, in 1603, did little to appease the situation.
Newcastleton, known locally as Copshaw Holm,
is less than three miles from the current border
between Scotland and England. It cradles the Liddel
Water and is the largest settlement in Liddesdale.
For many centuries Liddesdale was at the front line
in the wars between England and Scotland. The
troubled history of Hermitage Castle, a massive
14th century fortification five miles to the north,
illustrates this conflict. The name Newcastleton,
contrary to what you might think, has nothing to

do with the jolly Geordie city of Newcastle. It originates from a settlement called Castleton that grew up around Liddel castle sometime in the tenth century. The castle was destroyed in the 1300s and the original settlement disappeared. A little to the south of the original Castleton the Duke of Buccleuch planned and built Newcastleton as a hand loom weaving centre in 1793. It is a narrow village about a mile long and a couple of hundred yards wide. Its unusual design gave the residents maximum access to the Liddel Water. The village centers on Douglas Square with shops dotted along the main street. Liddesdale Heritage Centre and Museum is housed in the old Townfoot Kirk located at the south end of the village. It is run by the Liddesdale Heritage Association and covers the history of Liddesdale and its people. It is open daily from 1.30 pm to 4.30 pm, Easter to the end of September, except Tuesdays when it is closed. The village is also well known for its Traditional Music Festival, which happens on the first weekend in July. According to Professor Plumpton the celebrated folk-rock combo Steeleye Span commemorate the village in a song entitled "Copshaw Holme Fair", how he came by this information remains a mystery to me.

We headed south west out of Newcastleton up the B6357 then turned left at the signpost for Dykecrofts and followed the road for a mile to reach the trailhead. We walked down a winding path and crossed over a little bridge that spans the Linns burn. We then proceeded up a hill through an avenue of magnificent Norway Spruce trees. As we walked through this beautiful forest I could hear the faint, ceaseless, cracking sounds that are the constant soundscape of any living forest. It occurred to me that in the great outdoors you rarely come across complete silence. It is indeed true that nature abhors a vacuum.

At the top of the hill we came to a T-junction and there before us was the object of our quest. It is a very large wedge shape rock, rounded at its top, standing upright like the tail of an aeroplane. It is approximately 10ft tall by 5ft wide by 4ft thick and I would estimate that it would weigh about four tons. It seems to be made from some form of granite. The most distinguishing feature is the 9-inches diameter hole that cuts through it. The object is positioned in such a way that a person looking through the hole facing south is in fact looking towards England. Conversely if they look through the other way they will be looking at Scotland.

On one side, facing the north inscribed in old Scots, using a rather formal font, is the song 'Auld Lang Syne' by Scotland's favourite son, Robert Burns. On the opposite side is 'Jerusalem' by William Blake.

On the edge near the bottom there is the clue to the Mystery of the Seven Stanes. It looks like this.

Once again, dear readers, the dashes represent letters, which I have deliberately omitted. In case you have an attack of forgetfulness I would recommend that you take a note of the letters found and put them in the appropriate place at the back of this publication.

After examining the object closely I asked Professor Plumpton what his thoughts were and after a contemplative pause he replied.
"Well this it is indeed a rum do. Stones with holes in them like this one have always been associated with the art of healing. The most famous example is Men-an-tol, also known as the Crick Stone, near

Madron in Cornwall. These types of stones were used to heal lots of different kinds of illnesses through ceremonial rituals. Babies were passed through them three times as a cure for rickets, a common disease of infancy in the past.

He paused then continued.

"The choice of songs is very interesting considering the object's location. We are, after all, near what is now considered to be the official border of Scotland and England. Although in the past the location of that border was always in a state of flux. Therefore at one time this spot could have been considered to be the official border."

I concurred and he continued.

"You could say that 'Auld Lang Syne' is the quintessential Scottish song and likewise 'Jerusalem' could be seen as the equivalent quintessential English song. I would therefore deduce that the location and text are very significant to the object's intended purpose."

After a pause he smiled and said

"I have fond memories of singing 'Jerusalem' at my old school. Did you know that I went to a boarding school in England?"

I had suspected as much, but for the sake of civility I replied in the negative, then further enquired

"So Professor you know the song well?"

"Yes" he said.

"It's one of my favourite hymns. The words as you probably know are by England's revered mystic poet William Blake and the tune is by an old Etonian who went by the, somewhat long-winded, name of Sir Charles Hubert Hastings Parry. The words are taken from Blake's short poem entitled "And Did Those Feet In Ancient Time" The poem was inspired by the, rather far-fetched, story which describes Jesus, as a young man, accompanied by Joseph of Arimathea, visiting the ancient town of Glastonbury in England. The line about the satanic mills is generally seen as a reference to the devastation of nature caused during the industrial revolution. I always thought that the literal interpretation of the song was something of an irrelevance. The important thing is the inspirational qualities that it imbues in the singer or the listener Even though Blake cloaks his message in layers of protestant mysticism he is really talking about the universality of man. Human beings whether they be English, Scots or of indeterminate lineage, can come together and build a New Jerusalem, a heaven on earth. In the hermetic tradition, this momentous task would be referred to as, carrying

out the 'Magum opus' The Great Work.

I agreed, then after walking around the monolith said

"In fact 'Auld Lang Syne' has similar sentiments but puts it in a more direct fashion. The title roughly translated into English means 'Days Gone By'. As I am sure you are aware it is always sung at midnight on Hogmanay, or as the English would say, New Years Eve. This perhaps accounts for the fact that very few people know all the words of the song. If you can remember anything at that particular moment of the year you are either insane or you are a very brave man indeed."

At this remark Professor Plumpton nodded his head in agreement, so I continued.

"It is sung to a misty-eyed melody taken from an old Scots folk tune. The song in essence talks about friendships in the past that will never be forgotten. In this respect it could be seen as a unification of humanity spanning lifetimes. I suspect that it's this sentiment that has made it so universally popular today."

I then asked Professor Plumpton.

"So you would agree with me that the objects proximity to the border is significant?

"Yes without a doubt." He replied.

"The fact that the Scottish song is on the Scottish side facing England and the English song is on the English side facing Scotland, I believe is very significant."

As we stood there examining the edifice I thought I could feel a spot of rain on my forehead but I ignored it. I then asked Professor Plumpton what he thought the raison d'être of the object could be. "Well that's a big question. It seems to me that it's a bit like a challenge or a battle cry. Perhaps, unlike in days of old when you would attack your enemy with weapons made from steel, here it's like attacking them with poetry. There may be a lesson in this for us all. After all would it not be better to taunt an opponent with poetry as apposed to tanks and guns."

"Indeed." I agreed

"The United Nations could hold a strictly observed singing competition, where two countries in dispute could settle their differences. I could imagine in the future poets being treated like kings, as they would

in fact be the currency of the next arms race."
We both laughed at this preposterously idealistic
idea.

As Professor Plumpton measured and sketched
the object a mountain biker came out of nowhere,
like a greyhound of the forest, and stopped in front
of us. He was not a young chap probably in his
early forties and he was wearing an anarchy t-shirt.

Professor Deeson points out the Inscription
to an Anarchist Biker.

I wondered if that was the right kind of attire for
a man of his age to adopt. I distinctly remember
thinking, when I was a student, that anarchy was a
bit out of order. Anyway, he asked us what we were
doing, and I explained the situation to him then

pointed out the inscription. This seemed to satisfy his curiosity and made him smile. He then whipped out a mobile phone and asked me if I would be so kind as to take a picture of him standing next to the stone. After some instruction on the usage of the device I obliged the chap and he departed as quickly as he arrived.

As we walked back to the car, sure enough, as Mrs. Postlethwaite had predicted, a light shower appeared on the horizon. Five minutes later it had the audacity to throw itself, with fury, onto poor Professor Plumpton's head. I did the gentlemanly thing and never chastised him for forgetting his Boy Scout training. When we reached the Bentley the inscrutable Hargreaves seemed to have pre-empted this event as he produced a towel and gave it to the extremely wet professor. We retired to the comforting backseat of the car and Professor Plumpton produced a fine bottle of Napoleon brandy from a concealed cocktail cabinet, thoughtfully installed there by his late father. We shared a drink to warm our inner-souls. Near the end of our journey home, and near the end of the bottle of brandy, we thought as homage to the Bard we would sing 'Auld Lang Syne'. Unfortunately, even

though we had spent an hour looking at the lyrics of the song, we seemed to have forgotten most of the words. I could only conclude from this state of affairs that the brandy was somewhat stronger than I had appreciated. You have to hand it to old Rabby; only he could come up with a drinking song that manages to convey so much sentiment even though the singer can't remember the words. When we reached Edinburgh the rain had abated and our spirits had brightened considerably. We asked Hargreaves to drop us off near the Lawnmarket and we retired to Deacon Brodie's Tavern for a nightcap, to reflect on the days adventuring.

The Greyhound of the Forest.

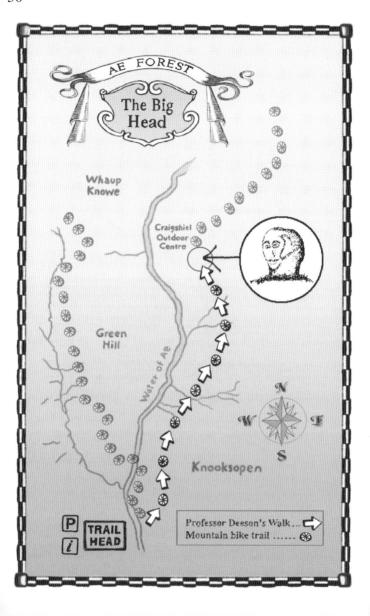

*Chapter Three*

## Ae Forest

# The Big Head

*Where Professor Deeson discovers the source of today's bicycle, breathes some divine air and confronts a big head.*

On the third day of our expedition to uncover the Mystery of the Seven Stanes we set off early from the Athens of the North and glided south down the M74. As Hargreaves maintained a steady seventy five miles per hour, we passed a number of cars with mountain bikes attached to their roofs. I must say, if it had not been for our glorious quest, I would probably never have noticed them. It is strange to see these machines, these greyhounds of the forest, being propelled along on the top of a car. Like horses being dragged along in horseboxes they seemed to be rather docile, almost peaceful as they are transported along. Their appearance is far removed from the speed-obsessed animals they become when let loose in the forest. What an amazing thing a bicycle is. It is an incredibly efficient machine converting fuel, in the form of

human muscle-power, into glorious speed. If God had put wheels on human beings, I doubt if he could have done a better job. Speed is an addictive drug, mix it with a hint of danger and you have a heady elixir. The Italian futurist poets were obsessed by it and stated in their manifesto 'We declare that the splendour of the world has been enriched by a new beauty: the beauty of speed.'

After turning off the motorway at Moffat on to the A701 we reached the village of Ae, which is around 10 miles north of Dumfries. Its strange name is taken from the Water of Ae, a tributary of the river Annan. Ae is thought to derive from 'ey' the Gaelic word for river. The village was built in the 1940s to house forestry workers and was the first purpose-built 'Forest village' in Scotland. It has a school, a shop and a pub called the Woodman's Bar. It also has the distinction of having the smallest place name in Scotland and probably in the United Kingdom.

Ae Forest, like all the forests we visited on our glorious quest, is managed by The Forestry Commission. According to their publicity 'It has been developed for public access and there are miles

of forest trails and paths giving access to all parts of this man-made woodland for walkers, cyclists and horse riders.' The forest acts as a drainage basin for the Water of Ae and encompasses the magnificent Loch Ettrick. Within this fine forest you can visit an open air collection of historic forestry ploughs, which I have been reliably informed is a must see experience for anyone interested in old forestry ploughs.

Ae forest has the designation of being a 'Priority Woodland' for Red Squirrel conservation. As I am sure you know, the red squirrel is the native of these blessed isles and in recent times has had a bit of a hard time of it competing against its American cousin, the Grey Squirrel. As we arrived at the trailhead, which is just past Ae village, Hargreaves said he saw one of these beautiful little creatures. Unfortunately neither Plumpton nor myself could confirm this sighting.

Red Squirrel not its American cousin.

We left Hargreaves at the trail head and advanced into the darkness and solitude of this mystical forest. As I walked along I became aware of the immortal life contained within it. Every tree sending its roots and branches forth in search of nourishment, every leaf jostling for position in order to catch the optimum amount of sunlight. Walking along, I had a definite sense of being contained within a living organism. A completely balanced ecosystem where each dead leaf or branch becomes nourishment for the living being, which is the forest. There is nothing wasted in a forest, nothing is discarded. Everything is recycled to become part of the living, balanced, ecosystem. In fact you could say that even the foresters who manage the forest are now an integral part of that ecosystem. As they selectively fell trees, they allow new growth to replace them, thus maintaining continuity and balance.

As we headed towards the object of our quest, six mountain bikers passed us and Professor Plumpton remarked,

"You know Professor Deeson, this sport of mountain

biking does add a bit of colour and diversity to these forests. It also does no harm to the living trees, as can be seen from the well maintained trails."

I agreed wholeheartedly, then explained that I considered mountain biking in forests an interesting development in the management of the planet's resources. As humans have more leisure time due to the mechanisation of the workplace they will continue to find diverse ways of filling that leisure time. I remember as a boy I would watch lots of wildlife films on my father's black and white television and they would always thoroughly depress me. At the end of these programmes there would always be the obligatory announcement that in the future such and such a species will be hunted out of existence by big game hunters. As it turned out nowadays there are numerous big game reserves in Africa that are thriving as a result of regulated hunting. The hunting brings revenue into the reserve and allows it to be managed properly for the benefit of all concerned. The diversification of forest management can only be seen as a good thing. It should be applauded as long as the activities promoted do not infringe on the integrity of the forests. After all, as The Forestry Commission is a

government body, the forests they manage belong to everyone. People should certainly be encouraged to use them.

"Quite so." Professor Plumpton agreed, then asked.

"How do you think this diversification will develop in the future?"

After a moments thought I replied.

"It is difficult to predict, after all twenty years ago it would have been preposterous to suggest that people would be having lots of fun riding their bikes through the forest. Perhaps in the future, tourists will be spending the night in beautiful tree houses constructed amongst the comforting branches of solid oak trees."

As we continued to walk towards the object of our quest Professor Plumpton remarked.

"I think it is quite appropriate that they should be speeding along these trails on their amazingly fast bicycles. As you probably know, Professor, Dumfriesshire has a good claim to be the birthplace of the bicycle."

I was rather surprised by this comment, so enquired.

"In what regard can Dumfriesshire make such a

claim Professor?"

"Well," he continued,

"I remember hearing the story from my father, who incidentally was a keen inventor. He spent years developing a circular slide rule device which, unfortunately, came to nothing when Sir Clive Marles Sinclair invented the first electronic pocket calculator. Anyway Father told me about Kirkpatrick McMillan, a Dumfriesshire man, who put together what is generally agreed to be the first peddled bicycle. McMillan was a modest Scottish blacksmith who was born in 1813 at Keir Mill, which is about 12 miles northeast of Dumfries. In 1839 he used his blacksmith skills to add pedals to a velocipede and thus created the first pedal-driven bicycle. Unfortunately he never thought of patenting his invention and the world would probably have forgotten all about him if it was not for an article in the Glasgow Herald printed in 1842. It reported that an accident occurred in which a gentleman from Dumfriesshire bestride a velocipede of ingenious design knocked over a pedestrian in the Gorbals village and was fined five British shillings for the crime. What Kirkpatrick McMillan would have made of these magnificent modern machines, these greyhounds of the forest,

we will never know but I tend to think he would have wholeheartedly approved of their immaculate engineering."

"Quite so," I agreed. "I'm sure old McMillan would be amazed and delighted with them."

As we continued our walk we began to climb a large hill and sensing our closeness to the unspoilt heavens above I was aware of the purity of the air. There is something to be said about noticing the very air you breathe, when a bracing inhalation exhilarates the spirit and puts one in a good mood. It is indeed surprising how we get used to breathing the chemical soup that is laughingly referred to as 'air' by our fellow city-dwellers. It is only when you come to places like this that you realise what air is supposed to taste like. That sweet breathe of life.

After walking along for about two miles, we found ourselves high above the valley of the Water of Ae. The valley is covered in Sitka spruce with a light sprinkling of Larch. Far to the left you can just make out the Solway Firth. To the right of it there is a forest road which when touched by the sun, looks remarkably like a large waterfall. At the

top of the hill just before the entrance to a dark brooding forest we were confronted with the third object in our quest.

It takes the form of a large monolith with a face carved into its surface. It is 6ft tall by 4ft 6-inches wide by 4ft 6-inches thick and probably weighs about five tons. This face seems to be staring over the glorious panoramic view set before us. The carving is somewhat primitive in style but nevertheless it is quite charming in its silent demeanour. It is rather reminiscent of the face of a Sheela-na-Gig figure those female fetish exhibitionist figures found all over the British Isles and Ireland. It is said that their purpose is to ward off evil and death.

Carved around the face is a very beautiful verse written in English. It reads.

> 'But still it satisfies my soul
> to hear the spruce and the wind
> They speak together like sister and brother
> and use such beautiful wind-wild words
> deep in the forest, deep in the forest.'

Professor Plumpton remarked,
"I love the idea of the wind talking to the trees. It is a wonderful evocation of the solitude of this location."
"Yes." I agreed.
Who would have thought we would come across a talking head in this marvellous location.

On one side of the object, near the bottom, you will find the clue to the Mystery of the Seven Stanes. It looks like this.

Once again the dashes represent letters. I would suggest that you take a note of these three letters

and insert them in the appropriate place at the back of this publication. Then send in your form to get a tree planted in your name.

As we returned to the car park it occurred to me how privileged we are to live in a country which has such a diversity of scenery. In relation to the scale of the big wide world Scotland is a tiny little place, yet you can climb magnificent mountains, swim in splendid lochs, traipse through incredibly dense forests and safely get back home for tea, all in a day. It is a wonderful country to converse with the spirit of nature and there is no doubt that our lives are enriched by it when we return to the comfort of our own homes.

Kirkpatrick McMillan's Dream

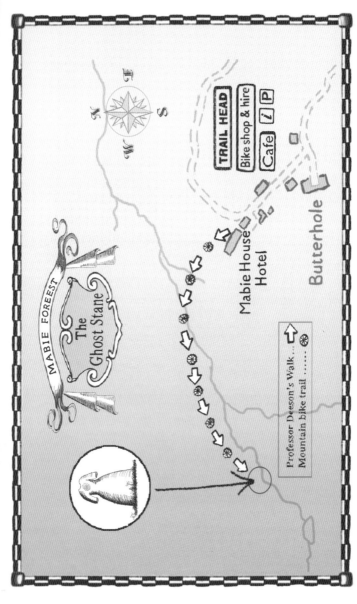

Chapter Four

## Mabie Forest

# The Ghost Stane

*Where Professor Deeson consumes a delightful game pie, has an epiphany and manages to avoid a beastly scene.*

On the fourth day of our adventure my colleague Professor Plumpton and I sat in the back seat of his Bentley as his trusted chauffeur, Hargreaves, drove us through the elegantly proportioned streets of Scotland's majestic capital. Hargreaves pointed the immaculate vehicle's three and a half tons of precision engineering towards Dumfries and we were once again on our merry way towards the fair and glorious border country.

Having spent the previous night in the bar of the Deaf Poet discussing the merits of Pre-Raphaelite drawing with an old university friend, it was my intention to have a snooze on the journey. Alas when we hit the motorway Professor Plumpton seemed to become rather excited about our forthcoming excursion and insisted on producing

maps explaining where today's object of curiosity was lurking. As I did not want to put a damper on the old boy's ardour I feigned a degree of enthusiasm and allowed him to brief me on our mission.

The object in question was the fourth to be uncovered by those chaps at The Forestry Commission. It is located in the Forest of Mabie, which is four and a half miles south of Dumfries. It was found in an area between the National Costume Museum of Scotland and the ruin of the romantically named Sweet Heart Abbey. The stone object was reported to be very large and contained an inscription, thus linking it to the other six artefacts under our investigation.

Passing through Dumfries the impenetrable Hargreaves suggested that it would be a sound idea to find a local hostelry in order to procure some lunch before we entered the forest. As we always tried to encourage Hargreaves' initiatives we agreed. He then took us to a pretty little village, five miles south of Dumfries, known as New Abbey. To the southwest of this picture book village the land rises steadily to the summit of Criffel. While a little over a mile to its east a small river with the rather

eccentric name of the New Abbey Pow flows into the estuary of the River Nith. The village has great charm and character and boasts a shop and a post office. It also has a second major visitor attraction, after Sweetheart Abbey, the New Abbey Cornmill. Both these attractions are run by Historic Scotland and I have been reliably informed that it is possible to purchase joint tickets if you have the notion to visit. We took this opportunity to visit one of the village's delightful eating establishments. I had a sumptuous game pie with roast potatoes and Professor Plumpton had a weighty ploughman's platter. We washed down our gastronomic treats with a couple of shandys.

This fine lunch raised our spirits and we proceeded towards Mabie Forest. The trailhead is at the site of the wonderful Mabie House, the former home to the Keswick family. We enter the forest of Mabie with the conviction of Stanley on his divine pursuit of the saintly Livingstone. There is something rather magical about a delightful walk in a forest. Perhaps it is the recollection of all those mysterious fairy tales we consumed as children. These stories always portrayed forests as magical

places, enchanted kingdoms that could seduce children into strange worlds of freaky goblins and illusive fairies. As you walk along a forest path your eye seeks out features. Sometimes it's a bird or a stone; sometimes it's a root or a branch. The general atmosphere of lush green foliage transports your mind away from the hustle and proverbial bustle of everyday life and rejuvenates your psyche.

As we passed by the little Mabie Burn I looked down and had something akin to an epiphany. The effervescent bubbles in one's first gin and tonic of the day could never compare with the rapture I experienced when gazing at that little burn. I watched it hurtle down the hill, playfully caressing every polished stone, as it continued on its God given journey towards the loving embrace of the all-encompassing open sea.

After a short walk we came to a misty glade where the little burn turns a corner and is surrounded by Beech trees, Scots Pines and Oaks. It is a rather enchanted bower and nestled within it lay our quarry. I can truthfully say it was a wonder to behold. Framed by the lush greenery of the forest, its whiteness

conveyed an unworldly persona. It shimmered like
a ghostly apparition, as if containing an inner light
source buried deep within its colossal mass.

It is approximately 14 feet high and something
like six feet wide and it appears to have been carved
from a solid chunk of white marble. It probably
weighs something in the region of two and a half
tons. When I asked Professor Plumpton what kind
of marble he thought it could be I was somewhat
surprised by his reply. He was of the opinion that
it was more likely to be alabaster. He deduced this
from the fact that it had a slight transparency and
further postulated that a stone of its size could only
have been quarried in the town of Alabastron in
Egypt. I found this suggestion to be preposterous,
but for the sake of avoiding a beastly scene I
resisted the urge to contradict him. I thought it best

to let the wonders of science provide us with an impeccable unbiased answer so I suggested that we should take a sample and have the university lab analyse it.

The object was certainly foreboding but appeared to possess an element of hidden magnificence. It looked something like a tall figure whose features have been obliterated by the passage of time. As if carved by some unknown hand many moons ago then subjected to the ravages of endless sand storms. Like the magnificent sphinx in the Valley of the Kings, what stood before us was a ghost of its former self. Just below the place where the figure's head would be, if it had one, there is a carved lace like solar symbol.

At the back of the figure, near the bottom, you will find the expected clue. It looks like this

Once again the dashes represent letters and if you are intending to complete the puzzle I would suggest you take a note of them at the appropriate place at the back of this publication.

We both stood there, perfectly still like the surrounding trees, as if consumed by a large cloud of wonderment or to be more accurate, a large cloud of befuddlement. Who could have produced such an artefact and what on this earth was the purpose of its manufacture?

I asked Professor Plumpton if he thought the location of the object, its site-specifity, could give us a clue to its purpose.

He replied,

"Sweetheart Abbey, which is roughly eight miles south of Dumfries and a stone's throw from where we are now standing, was a Cistercian monastery founded in 1275 by Dervorgilla of Galloway, who was the daughter of Alan, Lord of Galloway. She founded the abbey church in memory of her husband John de Balliol whose embalmed heart was placed in a casket of ivory and silver and buried alongside her when she died. As a tribute to her love for her husband, the monks in the abbey thereafter called it Dulce Cor or Sweetheart Abbey. Unfortunately, over time, both graves have been lost. The Order of Cistercians (Latin: *Cistercienses*), meaning white monks, is derived from the colour of their habit, over which a black scapular or apron was worn.

It is a Roman Catholic order of enclosed monks. The basic premise of Cistercian life was a return to a literal observance of the Rule of Saint Benedict. Rejecting the developments the Benedictines had made, the Cistercians tried to reproduce life exactly as it had been in Saint Benedict's time, sometimes going beyond it in their austerity. Their most obvious practice was the return to manual labour. During the Protestant Reformation the Cistercians were badly affected by Henry VIII's Dissolution of the Monasteries, and consequently Sweetheart Abbey suffered dreadfully."

"Indeed," I replied, stemming Plumpton's eloquent flow,

"But let me ask you again old chap, do you think the object's nearness to the abbey has any significance?"

This produced a rather embarrassing silence, but after some prompting the Professor replied

"Well no, I doubt it. In fact as the monks were into piety in a big way I doubt they would be willing to spend their time importing this magnificent block of stone and carving it into some kind of effigy of themselves. It would in fact be completely out of character."

"Quite so." I replied. "My sentiments exactly."

He then suggested that the object may have some connection to the costume museum. I thought this kind of remark hardly worthy of his position in academia. Sometimes there is a lack of common sense in Professor G.R Plumpton's remarks that pains me. For the sake of the task at hand and a quiet life. I answered.

"No, there is no chance of that: the artefact is far too old and the costume museum is a relatively new addition to the landscape. It is housed in the 19th-century Shambellie House and, according to its publicity, gives a vivid snapshot of former lives through a series of room settings. I remember visiting it many years ago, when it first opened. I was dragged along by my Great Aunt Agatha. She had donated some rather fine Victorian dresses and, even though she had given them to the nation, the old girl seemed to think it was her duty to keep an eye on them. Why she took me along, I will never know. I remember thinking at the time that woman's dresses, especially of the Victorian period, held no interest for me. After all I was a young boy, more concerned with marbles and spitfires. Having said that, I do recall being rather taken by some exquisitely embroidered christening gowns in the museum's collection.

The lace carving on the object is probably derived from whitework, which is a form of early lace making where white thread is used to stitch patterns onto a white muslin material. Ayrshire was famous for producing this kind of work and there is a fine collection of it in Dumfries Museum.

Professor Plumpton produced a large tape measure and, with great exactitude, measured the object. He then proceeded to make some sketches of the entity in his notebook and I took this opportunity to use my trusty Leica camera to take a few snaps. This documentation would be invaluable when finally collating our data. Ever since we encountered the first object I had the suspicion that we would only approach their real meaning when we had recorded all seven accurately. Only then, after subjecting the problem to our razor sharp academic scrutiny, could we postulate a reasonable working theory as to what their purpose was.

After the deed of recording was done we trooped back to the car where I deduced that old Hargreaves seemed to be rather pleased with himself. He had the look of a man who had just completed the Times crossword.

It was now five o'clock and Professor Plumpton was in a hurry to get back to Auld Reekie. He had very kindly booked a table for us at the Cloven Hoof, one of the city's finest eating establishments. He was particularly keen to arrive on time, as he did not want to endure the wrath of the Maitre D who was supposedly a leading light in a particular secret society, well established in the city.

Old Hargreaves put his foot down and did not break too many bylaws in his quest to deliver us there on time. Looking at his, now rather sombre demeanour you would never have believed that the old goat was a bit of a whiz kid in his youth. Professor Plumpton told me that he had once taken part and nearly won the Le Mans twenty four hour. After our dinner, which was first rate, we decided to retire to Cob's Club for Gentlemen in order to plan the next part of our expedition.

# DALBEATTIE FOREST
## The Heart

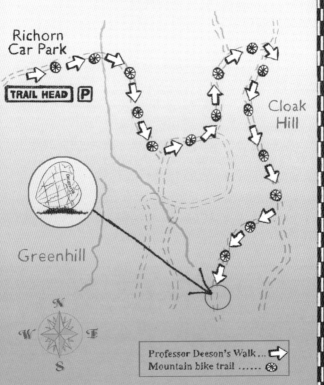

Richorn Car Park

TRAIL HEAD [P]

Cloak Hill

Greenhill

N W E S

Professor Deeson's Walk ...
Mountain bike trail ...... ⊛

*Chapter Five*

# Dalbeattie Forest

# The Heart Stane

*Where Professor Plumpton almost recovers from a bad dose of the theatre before he proceeds to the heart of the matter, and the intrepid Professor Deeson waits for the fairies to dance.*

We left the Athens of the North on the fifth day of our glorious quest at ten o'clock on a fine, bright sunny morning. Sitting in the back seat of Professor Plumpton's Bentley I noticed he looked a little green behind the gills, so I enquired,

"Are you all right old chap?"

"Yes" he replied. "Just a little queasy, I'm afraid I had a bit of a late night."

"Really." I enquired further. "Pray tell, what did you get up to?"

"Well I met an old friend who is something of a name in the theatre business and he suggested we take in a play.

"Really" I replied with amazement, wondering what could have possessed the man.

"Yes," he continued.

"Unfortunately it was a very dull affair, three men

sitting in a white box on bentwood chairs mincing on intolerably and getting very exited in the process of doing so. After hours of this infernal theatrical torture my friend and I finally escaped to the bar. It turned out that the play was supposed to be a radical interpretation of the Scottish play, which was certainly news to me. My friend, who has great experience of this kind of theatrical excess, explained to me that the three bentwood chairs doubled up as the three witches. In a effort to forget the evening's so called, entertainment we went to the Waverly Bar and inevitably one thing led to another and I got home in the wee small hours of this morning."

I shook my head, then replied.

"It sounds as if you have been through the mill old chap."

"Indeed Professor." he said.

"It was a somewhat beastly experience."

Even though I find it hard to sympathise with a man who gives himself a sore head, I did feel some empathy for poor Plumpton. Personally I strenuously avoid any forays into theatre-land. I then asked him if he thought he would be all right for today's jaunt.

"Oh yes." he replied. "I'll be fine, I just need a little time to regain my pep, I'm sure the forest air will work wonders on me."

We arrived in Dalbeattie, which is set in the beautiful Urr valley and is surrounded by forest and woodland. It is a modest, quaint town of about 4,000 people with its streets laid out on a grid-plan. It was founded in 1793 as a mill town and coastal port making use of the natural basin where the Dalbeattie Burn enters the River Urr. It was a famous granite quarrying centre. Granite from Dalbeattie was used to build parts of Windsor Castle. Today this heritage can be clearly seen as most of the town's houses and buildings are built with local granite. The name Dalbeattie is derived from a Gaelic term, Dail Bheithe, meaning 'Valley of the Silver Birch.' The local tourist board came up with the somewhat dubious slogan 'Dalbeattie, the Town of Hard Granite and Warm Hearts'. In the museum at Southwick Road you can learn about the town's best-known historical figure, Lieutenant William McMaster Murdoch who was the First Officer of the ill-fated White Star liner RMS Titanic. Unfortunately the poor chap went down with his ship in 1912 when she struck an iceberg

on her maiden voyage. The museum attempts to tell the real history of the man, who was a hero and not a cowardly villain, as portrayed in the 1997 James Cameron movie. You will find the museum open from April to the end of October, Monday to Saturday from 11am to 4pm and Sundays from 2pm to 4pm. Entrance is free, but of course donations are always welcome.

The RMS Titanic, no Cowardly villain.

The inscrutable Hargreaves, whom I suspect was thinking of his employer's fragile mental state, suggested that refreshments might be in order before we entered the forest. We agreed and proceeded to enter one of the town's fine hostelries. I had a whisky and ginger ale and Professor Plumpton had a large glass of Iron Bru which I am sure, dear reader, you know is reputedly brewed from girders. Thankfully this sparkling draft seemed to restore some of the old boys depleted pep.

After our refreshment we left Dalbeattie driving south towards Colvend on the A710 and soon reached the trailhead at the Richorn car park. The northern end of Dalbeattie Forest is known as the Town Wood due to its position on the edge of Dalbeattie. The current forest was planted in the 1920s, and now extends six miles south to the village of Colvend. It has a diverse mixture of trees including mature broadleaves and a variety of conifers. It is said that there is a thriving population of red squirrels in Dalbeattie Forest, but alas as we walked past trees such as cherry, beech and hazel we never saw any bushy red tails or any scampering little red bodies whizzing past us.

As I walked though the forest listening to the rustling of leaves and crackling of twigs, I was struck by the natural architecture of the place. Strolling through the towering columns of this majestic woodland I was in awe of the passionate wonder of the forest's upward movement. There is no doubt that this transcendental natural landscape has a striking similarity to the interiors of gothic cathedrals with their robust columns and vaulted ceilings. Even the sun light filtering through the tree tops was reminiscent of stained glass windows

set high in cathedral walls. I was conscious of the underlying structures, which manifest themselves in the form of the living forest. It was as if I was walking through a temple to nature, a temple dedicated to the pulse of life, a temple which was the abode of some kind of ancient god or goddess. Fortunately before I was completely converted to a new-age form of Druid ideology we came to the object of our quest.

The object is surrounded by granite boulders and is overlooked by the site of an Iron Age hill fort. It is in the form of a large granite, probably Dalbeattie granite, heart. It sits on a natural plinth constructed from soil and is in clear view from a great distance. The heart measures 5ft 9-inches tall by 7ft 6-inches wide by 3ft 2-inches thick and weighs about 5 to 7 tons

At the back of the heart, near the bottom, you will find the expected clue. It looks like this.

Once again, the dashes represent letters and I would suggest you take a note of them at the appropriate place in the back of this publication.

The Heart lies on its side and has a map of the world carved into it. This map seems to have been distorted to show Scotland at the centre of the world. When you stand next to this colossal object you can see the village of Dalbeattie in the background and to its left you can see the Dalbeattie quarry, where just such a rock could have been quarried. As we examined the object I asked Professor Plumpton what he made of it.

"Well," he said scratching his head, "the carving is very interesting. When we see a generic world map we assume it is an accurate representation of world geography. This is a strange assumption as the map we are used to seeing is in fact quite distorted. If the world was mapped geographically correctly it would be very different. For example Africa would actually be much larger than it is normally displayed. The world map we see today is something of a political map. Likewise here, on this object, Scotland and therefore Dalbeattie appears to be at the centre of the world.

"Yes," I agreed", then asked,

"Do you have any other thoughts on this wonderful object.

"Well," he replied, "aesthetically, I find it to be an extremely pleasing object. The heart, as I am sure you are aware Professor, was historically seen as the seat of the human mind, the abode of the soul, the centre of one's spiritual and emotional being. It was also thought to be the organ where the process of thinking took place. This is a strange notion for a person in the twenty-first century to comprehend. We think of ourselves as being positioned in our heads sitting on top of our bodies. It is difficult for us to think of ourselves existing in the centre of our chests. Nevertheless the ancients noticed that in times of heightened emotions fear, love, excitement etc, the heart would speed up and they concluded that their core being must reside in their heart. Even though we now know that the brain is where thinking occurs, this notion of the heart being responsible for emotions still lingers in the common psyche. This accounts for common expressions like, 'hand on heart', 'have a heart', 'giving your heart to another', 'wearing your heart on your

sleeve'etc. It's quite interesting that sophisticated modern human beings should still feel the need to separate emotions and intellect as if, somehow, they are different entities."

"Quite so", I agreed, then added, "this kind of heart mythology is definitely a throwback from the ancient world. The Egyptians held the heart in great reverence, as they thought it was the only organ that preceded them into the afterlife. It is stated in the Egyptian Book of the Dead that when a person is being judged, after they die, their heart is balanced against the feather of Mat'at, who was the goddess of law and order. If that person's heart was heavier than the feather it would have been consumed by the demon known as Ammit, who had the body of a lion and the head of a crocodile. Obviously as this meant an end to the progressive evolution of the person's soul, any self respecting Egyptian would want to avoid this outcome." After a pause where I contemplated the incredible beauty of the surrounding landscape I continued.

"The Aztecs also had a fixation with the organ; it was prominent in their human sacrifice ceremonies. The head priest would use a stone knife to remove the heart of the poor chap being sacrificed and

place it on the alter as a token of goodwill to the gods. It is written that in the reign of the mighty Montezuma there was an occasion where 12,000 hearts were sacrificed in this way. All taken from captured enemy soldiers, of course. In those days no-one had heard of the Geneva Convention."

"The past is indeed a strange country," Professor Plumpton remarked, then continued,

"The word heart can also refer to the centre of things, as in the expression

'Getting to the heart of the matter' and as we are in a forest, in relation to trees, heartwood is the wood found at the centre of a tree.

"That is true." I answered. "I was just thinking that this fine stone heart set before us reminds me of our Auld Reekie's Heart of Midlothian. The cobblestone mosaic situated on the pavement to the west of St Giles Kirk. It supposedly depicts the centre of Midlothian but actually represents the position of the 15th century tollbooth that was the location of many a public execution. There is a fine tradition of Edinburgh citizens spitting on it as they pass. It is said to have been begun by members of the criminal fraternity who were cursing the power of the governing authorities. Today however every one seems to partake in the ritual, presumably to

gain luck in their law abiding activities. Of course since the local government boundary changes of 1974, Edinburgh is not actually in Midlothian any more but, like a forgotten transplant organ, the heart still remains there.

"Yes," replied Professor Plumpton" That is a good point. I was thinking the same thing. You could say that The Heart of Midlothian is a representation of the soul of Edinburgh. If you are prepared to believe that a person has a soul, then why should a city, or a place or even a forest not have a soul? Aboriginal people all over the world certainly believe in such things.

The ancient Druids also thought it to be the case and today a lot of new-agers believe it to be so. In fact they go further, and believe that the world is one gigantic self regulating entity which has a soul, a spirit. The case for this idea is very well set out in Professor James Lovelock's book 'Gaia A New Look At Life On Earth'. Gaia of course is a reference to the Greek earth goddess."

After we both walked round the object pondering its meaning, I asked Professor Plumpton, "Do you think this stone heart could be a representation of the heart of Dalbeattie?"

"Yes," he replied enthusiastically.

"It would not be too unreasonable an assumption that this stone object could represent the heart or the soul of Dalbeattie. It is after all made of the same granite that made the town famous."

As I watched Professor Plumpton meticulously measure and sketch the stone heart, it occurred to me that a forest seems to be in a constant state of waiting. As if the goddess of the forest, divine nature herself, had suspended her activities until every man, woman and child had left. Like when the fairy folk stop their dancing at the sound of human footsteps. I wondered what occurs in this enchanted realm when it is free from the logic of human consciousness.

We walked back to the car, and in no time at all we were gliding through the streets of Scotland's majestic capital. I asked Professor Plumpton if he cared to join me for a shandy, but, strangely, he declined my offer. This rejection surprised me as I had never known him to refuse any form of refreshment. I suspected that the poor chap had not quit totally recovered from the previous nights theatrical tomfoolery.

# The Gem Stane

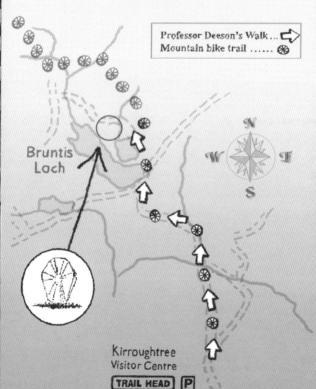

KIRROUGHTREE FOREST

Professor Deeson's Walk ... ➪
Mountain bike trail ....... ✳

Bruntis
Loch

Kirroughtree
Visitor Centre

TRAIL HEAD  P

*Chapter Six*

# Kirroughtree Forest

# The Gem Stane

*Where fearless Professor Deeson blows away some cobwebs, discovers an enchanted loch and recalls a very green encounter.*

On the sixth day of our glorious quest we drove south towards Newton Stewart. Three miles east of the town we turned left at Palnure and arrived at Kirroughtree visitor centre. The name Kirroughtree comes from the estate once owned by the Heron family whose ancestry can be traced back to the Norman Conquest. Around the year 1300 a Gerald Heron fought on the side of King Robert the Bruce, who rewarded him by granting him the rich lands of Kirroughtree. In 1719 Patrick Heron, a wealthy cattle trader, built Kirroughtree House, which still remains in Newton Stewart. This magnificent edifice was the Heron family home for many generations. After a change in ownership in 1952 it became a rather sumptuous hotel. The poet Robert Burns was a good friend of the Heron family and

paid several visits to the House. Having said that, old Rabby did get around this part of the world and you would be hard pressed to find anywhere he did not visit.

Kirroughtree Forest is a mixed woodland of broadleaves and conifers offering an ambience and charm unique to this quiet corner of Bonny Scotland. In the Forestry Commission Scotland Visitor Centre there is said to be fun for all the family, where you will find friendly staff who can offer you information on all of the forest's facilities. There is also a delightful tearoom that serves light meals and refreshments, as well as a variety of gifts if you happen to require that special souvenir of your trip.

After leaving Hargreaves in the car park we walked through a veritable cornucopia of lush green vegetation where I was told by a passing forester you can find a mix of wildlife, from roe deer to flocks of finches. The path soon took us deeper into the forest where the trees were mainly Sitka and Norway spruce. As we walked along I pondered what a wonderful environment a forest is. Its ambiance allows your imagination to feast

upon its multifaceted fragrances, its rustling twigs, its pulsating life beating within every rock and tree. There is nothing like a walk in the forest to blow away those urban cobwebs that invariably cling to your inner mind.

We soon came to Bruntis Loch, which sits like a gleaming amethyst in its surrounding picturesque landscape. This Loch was created in the nineteenth century to provide power for the nearby lead mines. Like a natural sorcerer it employs its fluctuating sparkling surface to enchant any passing viewer. Through the lush green of the forest's veil, situated in a small intimate space on the waters edge, we spotted the object of our quest. It is somewhat smaller than the previously encountered objects, but the artistry of its form endows it with an impressive aura. It's like a very large pinkish gemstone that stands like a sentinel to the silence of its surroundings. It is a rock of some

uniqueness, with its multifaceted planes giving it a rather futuristic appearance. It is 4ft tall by 3ft 6-inches wide, by 2ft thick and probably weighs about 2 tons. I asked Professor Plumpton what his first impressions were.

"Well," he said, it seems to be made out of a pink quartzite and if, as I suspect, it is Scottish in origin it is an extremely rare find. As I am sure you are aware Professor, all quartzite was originally sandstone, which has been forced by heat and pressure to re-crystallize into quartzite. This means it is an extremely hard stone and thus very resistant to weathering."

"Indeed." I replied, "it does seem to be very hard and its highly polished surfaces and flat planes certainly reinforce its gem-like appearance".

"Yes" Professor Plumpton agreed.

"It definitely has a jewel-like quality. If it was actually pure quartz of this colour and scale it would be a very valuable piece of rock. Pink or rose quartz is a traditional healing stone and is held in high regard in new-age circles. It is thought to be a powerful talisman due to its crystal formation that can supposedly align our body's harmonies. Crystal healers believe that quartz has the ability to receive and send out healing energy. Rose quartz is

known as love stone, which is thought to be very powerful at healing emotional stress. If this was pure quartz people, who believe in such esoteric magic, would be flocking here in the hope of getting their broken-hearts mended."

"Indeed." I remarked, wondering just where Professor Plumpton accumulated all this information.

"I suppose we can be thankful that it is not pure quartz then."

Professor Plumpton laughed, then said.

"Quite so Professor, we would have to beat off all those love sick souls with a stick."

As it is not my habit to denounce people with far-out ideas I tried not to encourage the Professor's jest but I could not quite contain a smile when imagining such a sight.

At the back of the gem, near the bottom, you will find the expected clue which looks like this.

Once again the dashes represent letters which you can put in the appropriate place at the back of this publication.

I asked Professor Plumpton if he thought the location of the object was relevant.

"Well," he said, "Creetown is not far from here and it is the home to an amazing Gem Rock Museum, which is the leading independent museum of its kind in the United Kingdom. It is a world renowned centre for all things gemstone. I have visited it and can tell you it is an Aladdin's Cave of glittering treasures. It is owned and run by Tim Stephenson and has been in the family for three generations. Perhaps there is some connection there.

"Do you really think so?" I asked, thinking it to be a rather tenuous link. He did not reply.

At this point as we were examining the object a somewhat over-friendly Australasian chap appeared on his mountain bike. He seemed to be rather inadequately equipped for the vagaries of the Scottish weather as he was only wearing a T-shirt, shorts and a pair of sandals. He asked what we were doing and I informed him of our glorious quest. As I was curious I asked him what he got out of this ingenious sport of mountain biking.

"Well mate," he replied, "it's a real thriller, a real buzz. When you're going along with the wind in your face and you don't know what's round the next

tree, it's a kick and a half. I guess it's the adrenaline rush. That's what gets you, it's a real buzz".

"Really." I replied, taken aback by the chap's enthusiasm and wondering if he was on some kind of drug, perhaps cocaine.

"Yeh man you should give it a go," he continued, "even an old codger like yourself would love it".

"Yes", I informed him, "I probably will give it a go, as you say. Perhaps I will do it tomorrow."

Thankfully this statement seemed to satisfy his Australasian get up and go attitude and after enthusiastically shaking my hand he jumped onto his bike and disappeared back into the depths of the forest.

Professor Deeson with an Australasian chap poorly prepared for the rigors of the Scottish weather.

Standing there in this wondrous setting, watching Professor Plumpton recording the object, I was taken in by all the abundant luxuriant growth surrounding us. This immense greenness reminded me of my aunt Christabell. She was a quirky old dear who, God bless her, managed to see her 98th birthday. Unfortunately as time went on the old girl became a bit doolally, and in the end the family had to put her into a nursing home. I remember visiting her with my mother one summer afternoon and taking her out for some fresh air. When we went outside all she could say was.

"Oh look, everything is so green, look everyone, everything is so green." She kept repeating it like a demented guru who has discovered a new mantra. "Everything is so green", she would say, "Everything is so green", over and over again.

God only knows what the old dear would have made of this place. It would, no doubt, have sent her into the greenest of green deliriums.

We headed back to the car park and Hargreaves drove us back to Edinburgh where I decided to make and early night of it and retired with Edward Gibbon's 'The Decline and Fall of the Roman Empire', which I would highly recommend as bedtime reading.

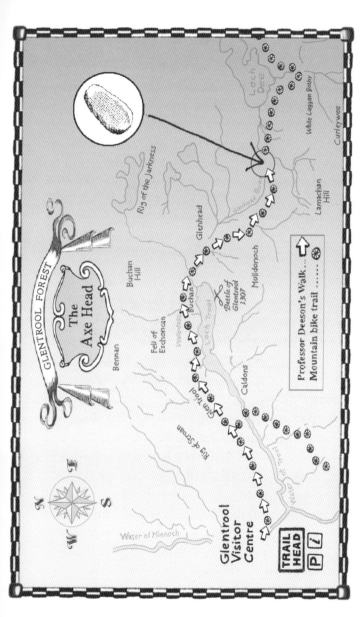

*Chapter Seven*

# Glentrool Forest

# The Axe Head

*Where the people of Newton Stewart are absolved of pagan rituals and an Irish giant is accused of being a litterbug.*

On the seventh and final day of our expedition we left Auld Reekie heading southwest on the A72 towards Newton Stewart. As we drove through the town Professor Plumpton informed me that in 1972 the celebrated cult horror movie The Wicker Man, directed by Robin Hardy and written by Anthony Shaffer, was filmed on location around these parts. He further informed me that it starred Edward Woodward alongside Christopher Lee and the beautiful Swedish actress Britt Ekland. At this point I would like to state that even though the film was shot around Newton Stewart it does not depict the activities of today's residents. The film depicts the townsfolk as being demented sex-loving pagans but I am reliably informed that the people of Newton Stewart would never get involved in such goings on.

The wicker man, nothing to do with the
good folks of Newton Stewart really.

From Newton Stewart we drove eight miles
north on the A714 heading towards Girvan. After
Bargrennan we took a right turn and followed the
signposts for Galloway Forest Park. We then came
to Glentrool Village which lies at the western end
of the Glen of Trool, 15 miles north of Newton
Stewart. It was built in 1954 to house workers who
were needed to plant the forest.

After we passed through the village we took the right fork and followed the signpost to Glentrool Visitor Centre. It is set in a beautiful corner of the forest next to the water of Minnoch and serves great food including a rare delicacy, the haggis toasty. Glentrool forest has been referred to as the Highlands in miniature and entertains the visitor with its wild beauty and intriguing history. It is also the host to Southern Scotland's highest mountain, the Merrick.

From the visitors centre we followed the trail and soon found ourselves in the quiet wilderness which is the heart of the Galloway hills. After a bracing five kilometre walk we came across the famous Bruce's Stone which commemorates the Battle of Trool in 1307. It is a fine solid monument to this historic event. The Stone was unveiled in 1929 at the 600th anniversary of King Robert the Bruce's death. The most magnificent thing about the monolith is it inspirational location. It is a wonderful example of finding the exact spot in a landscape to erect a monument, 'The Genius Loci', the precise location where the spirit of the place resides.

After admiring the monument we continued to walk up a somewhat arduous trek then entered a dense Spruce forest. As we approached the top of the hill we left the forest and were rewarded by the magnificent vista of Loch Dee. Superlatives fail me when trying to describe the outstanding beauty of this scenery. It must be one of the finest sights in the whole of Scotland. The loch, with its little islands, is set in the landscape like a precious jewel, as if the almighty himself had designed it to be photographed.

Just over the crest of a hill, found at the left hand side of the road, is the last object of our quest. It lies flat on the ground and is indeed a most beautiful object, obviously created by a real craftsman. It is 6ft 6-inches tall by 4ft wide by 1ft thick and probably weighs around two tons. The object's shape is reminiscent of a Neolithic axe-head but its massive scale would preclude it from ever being used as an axe. There have been many discoveries of large axe-heads, which were thought to be used as ceremonial objects. They would have been held by the king or shaman as a symbol of power, but to my knowledge one of this scale has never been

uncovered. If this object was ever used as an axe then it could only have been wielded by a giant. It is fashioned out of highly polished dark-greenish granite, which is veined with red, blood-like, flakes. The object's top surface is covered with an ancient runic text.

Embedded at the bottom of the runes is the clue, which looks like this.

Once again the dashes represent letters and if you are of a forgetful nature I would suggest you take a note of them at the appropriate place at the back of this publication.

When I asked Professor Plumpton for his views on the object he cleared his throat and in implacable academic tones stated

"Well Professor Deeson, as I am sure you know, the Runic alphabets are a set of related alphabets using letters known as Runes. They were most widely used to write Germanic languages before Christianisation replaced them with the Latin

alphabet. The Scandinavian version is known as, Futhark or fuþark, the name being derived from the alphabet's first six letters. The Anglo-Saxon variant is known as Futhorc. This inscription is in Anglo-Saxon Futhorc which means it could possibly date from the fifth century."

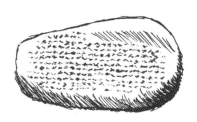

He then paused, so I encouraged him further by asking
"Indeed Professor and do you think you could translate it?"
"Yes certainly" he replied enthusiastically.
"As it happens I have studied this particular Runic form and I would be happy to translate it for you. Although you must remember in days of yore there was no standardisation of spelling or grammar so there may be some variation of meaning."
He then took a deep breath and recited the text with the eloquence of a contestant at The Royal National Mod.

'I am the wind that breathes upon the sea
I am the ocean wave
I am the murmur of the billows
I am the ox of the seven combats
I am the vulture of the rocks
I am a beam of the sun
I am the finest of plants
I am a wild boar of valour
I am a salmon in the water
I am a loch in the plain
I am a word of knowledge
I am the point of the lance in battle
I am the God who lights fire in the head
Who is it who throws light into
the meeting on the mountain?
Who announces the ages of the moon?
Who teaches the place where the sun makes his
bed?'

After a moment's contemplation I said
"Well that was indeed tremendous, a truly stunning
piece of ancient poetry. It is a remarkable evocation
of the omnipresent qualities of the Godhead."
"It is amazing," Professor Plumpton agreed.
"And I seem to recollect that I have heard it before
or at least something very similar to it. I can not

be sure until I look it up but I believe it to be an Irish poem. If I am correct it is a very ancient Irish poem, which makes me wonder how it got here?"

"Yes." I replied, "Good question."

"What we have here is a giant axe-head, or a giant's axe-head, inscribed with an extremely beautiful Irish poem. The combination of Irish poem and giant instantly suggest to me the often told story of Finn MacColl. As you will recall Professor, Finn MacColl was an Irish giant who had an argument with the Scottish giant named Ruiscare and challenged him to a fight. When Ruiscare protested that he couldn't fight because he could not swim across the Irish Sea MacColl threw him the Giants Causeway to help him across. When Ruiscare came over to Finn's house the Irish giant was dressed up as an 18-foot baby, and when the Scottish giant played with the child it bit his thumb off. Ruiscare was rather alarmed at this turn of events and wondered to himself, if this is what the babies are like in Ireland I don't want to meet the grownups. So he made a quick exit back to Scotland. Finn MacColl was enraged by this retreat and threw huge lumps of earth at him, one of them landed in the sea and is said to have become the Isle of Man."

After a pause I continued

"Perhaps there is a further part to this tale where old Finn also threw his axe at Ruiscare and it landed here. Of course this is just a flight of fancy on my part, it could never be determined with any finality. Nevertheless perhaps the makers of this object, some time in the very distant past, knowing the poem and knowing the story simply put the two together. It has to be remembered that history is a human creation; we make it up as we go along. Truths and legends are often mixed together and can sometimes lead to strange anomalies."

However the artefact ended up in this beautiful setting it cannot be denied that it is an object of exceptional beauty. After Professor Plumpton took detailed measurements we walked back down the hill to find Hargreaves in the car park. We made it back to Auld Reekie in plenty of time for tea.

# In Conclusion

Professor Plumpton and I spent the best part of three months collating the information gathered from our field trips. Even though it was an intellectually stimulating experience, alas at the end of that time we had accumulated more questions than answers. In effect, like most surveys of this nature, questions begat more questions. Perhaps, in the future after more detailed research is applied to the matter, these questions will be answered. As for now though, the best we can do is put forward an educated theory in the hope that it will suffice until someone else comes along with a better one.

Amongst many questions thrown up by the Mystery of the Seven Stanes is this fundamental one.

Are the seven objects discovered by The Forestry Commission actually connected to each other, beyond the fact that they contain clues to a puzzle?

After a great deal of deliberation I would conclude that there is no direct connection between each object other than the clues inscribed on them. My reasoning behind this conclusion is that the objects themselves are just too diverse both in nature and in timescale. I would further postulate that someone in the past came along and found a number of disparate objects and simply inscribed clues onto them. I'm afraid, at this moment in time, the identity of that person or persons is beyond my humble powers of deduction.

Each object has a separate identity which seems to relate to its own particular environment. A good example of this site-specificity is the object found at Newcastleton. With its reference to English and Scottish songs it directly relates to its location. This site-specific quality is repeated with each object, they all relate in some way or another to their immediate environment. It is only when these disparate objects are combined as a group by the inscribed clues, that a secondary meaning is revealed.

This idea of grouping together disparate objects, whose original purposes were completely independent of one another, is in fact a rather common occurrence in the world of archaeology. You just have to consider an old house that has been erected from fragments of previous buildings. That house will have its own personal history, but will also be an amalgamation of the previous buildings' histories. The seven objects are similar, as the clues found on them give them a secondary meaning thus allowing them to be viewed as one entity.

The seven clues when put into the puzzle make up a sentence. If you, dear reader, have completed the journey and found each clue you will now be aware of the contents of that sentence. The reason I have not revealed the contents here, is to allow all the budding archaeologists out there to enjoy the experience of personal discovery. Suffice to say the sentence connects all the seven objects and by default connects the seven forests.

Like the individual objects the individual forests we visited on our glorious quest are separate elements but when grouped together they can be seen as a single entity. Taking this idea further, if you connect the seven forests with every other forest in the world you can then hypothesize as to the purpose of forests in general. You can then ask why do forests exist and why are they an essential component of the living breathing Earth?

When you consider a forest's ecosystem, each individual leaf on a tree is part of that tree, each individual tree is part of that forest and each individual forest on planet Earth is part of the global forestry system. This global forest is an integral part of the world's ecosystem and without it human beings could not survive on this planet. The only conclusion any sane person can draw from this fact is, as a responsible planetary caretaker, we all have a responsibility to look after these magnificent environments, these wondrous enchanted kingdoms.

The Glorious quest to find the Mystery of the Seven Stains has been a marvelous adventure for both Professor Plumpton and myself. Apart from the obvious archaeological joy of discovering the seven objects we discovered something that we were both, shamefully, unaware of. We discovered the magnificent border country, an outstanding jewel in the crown of Bonny Scotland, without doubt one of the most beautiful regions on this, or any other, Earth. With its diverse rolling scenery and its magnificent vistas it is a heady elixir, an exotic tonic to cure any weary soul. Embedded deep within this magnificent scenery we also discovered the rich and almost unfathomable beauty which prevails within the seven forests. On many occasions, I must confess, superlatives simply failed me as I tried to describe the magnificence of these magical woodlands.

It could be said that perhaps a greater mystery, beyond the archaeological one, is the fact that more people are not aware of this magnificent border country. I don't normally venture into the world of the metaphysical but in the course of my journey it occurred to me that the journey itself might be more important than the end result. At times I had the impression that perhaps the seven objects were actually trying to tell me something beyond their physical presence. As if they were acting like windows or portholes allowing me to look beyond their mass and gaze in a cloud of wonderment at their surrounding landscapes. Perhaps the real answer to the Mystery of the Seven Stanes is encapsulated in the journey that you have to take to discover them. The search for their meaning is, as in life itself, simply a catalyst that allows us, as individuals, to explore our surroundings. Perhaps the real meaning of the quest is simply to allow the quest seeker the opportunity to discover the magical environment, which is the Seven Stanes Forests.

As the impenetrable Hargreaves once said,

*'Sometimes you have to get out of your Bentley before you can comprehend the breath-taking beauty of this magnificent world.'*

If you have visited The Seven Stanes and collected
the seven clues and would now like the Forestry
Commission to plant a tree in your name. Please
complete the puzzle overleaf.

# Fill in the missing inscriptions.

**The Meteorite**
Forest of Glentress

**The Border Stane**
Forest of Newcastleton

**The Big Head**
Forest of Ae

**The Ghost Stane**
Forest of Mabie

**The Heart**
Forest of Dalbeattie

**The Gem Stane**
Forest of Kirroughtree

**The Axe Head**
Forest of Glentrool

Send the completed puzzle to

Margaret Bryden
Forestry Commission Scotland
55/57 Moffat Road
DUMFRIES DG1 1NP

and get a tree planted in your name

| Name : | |
|---|---|
| Surname : | |
| Street : | |
| City : | |
| Post Code : | |

# With Thanks

Professor Ralph Deeson would like to take this opportunity to thank the following for their generous contributions to this book.

Forestry Commission Scotland, Ronnie Heeps, Gordon Young, Russell Coleman, Bevis Evans-Teush, Neil Ritchie, Ian Smith, Frank Plowright, Why Not Associates, Joanna Turner at Dumfries Museum, Mark Powers, Bob Young, Andy Altmann, Malin Wallen, Galloway Granite, John McKenzie, Jakki Service, Mark McCulloch, Gordon Christison, Frank Cluckie, Davie Cluckie, Davie McCleary, Stephen McCleary, Bobby Herris, Phil Addison, Lloyd and Barbara Siddle, Dot and Dave Baty, Brian Hill, Fiona and Brian at Campbells, Gordon Mckenzie at Tarmac Quarries, Richard Gardner, The Klingon Language Institute, Hans Børli, 'We own the Forests and Other Poems', Norvik Press and all the creatures plants and trees of all the forests in the world.